Mudlake

Written and illustrated by

B L Hinde

Mudlake
Text & Illustration copyright © B L Hinde 2007
Edited by Catherine White

First published and distributed in 2007 by Gatehouse Media Limited

Printed by Wallace Printers, Westhoughton

ISBN: 978-1-84231-027-4

British Library Cataloguing-in-Publication Data:
A catalogue record for this book is available from the British Library

Chapter 1

My name is Rob.

This is my tale.

Make of it what you will.

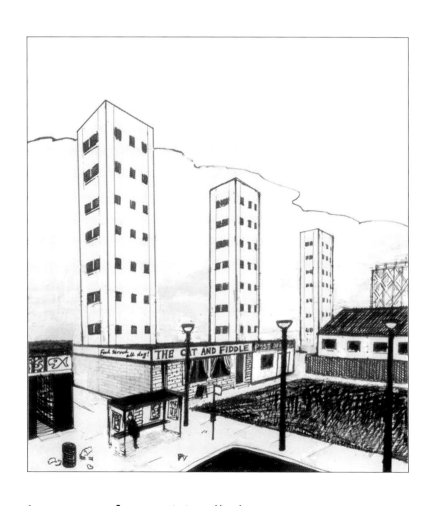

I came from Mudlake.

It was an estate at the end of town.

There was a post office and a pub.

There was a chip shop and a bus stop.

And there was a lake...

There were no jobs
and not much for a lad to do,
but take drugs and smash things up.
Me and Jake did a bit of that.

Jake was my best mate.

He was the same age as me.

We went to the same school.

But when I was 16, my dad got ill.
For his sake, I went into his trade.
That was when Jake fell in
with Dale and his gang.

Now Jake was not a bad kid.
He was a bit of a nut,
but his heart was in the right place.

But Dale was an ugly bit of work.
It was not a game with Dale.

There was a rape late one night.
It was Dale and his mates that did it.

I knew the victim and so did Jake.
Her name was Kim
and I know Jake liked her.

But Jake left when he saw
the plan Dale had.
He made up a tale
and said he had to go.

He ran away from it
and left Kim to her fate.
He rang the cops from a phone box.

He rang, but it was too late.

He made up a name.

He hung up.

He made a mess of it.

The rape case never came
before a judge.
Kim could not face it.
Kim could not face them.

She left Mudlake
and so did all her family.

Dale and his mates got away with it.
My uncle saw them in the pub.
Jake was not with them.

Chapter 2

Jake woke up late every day.

All he did was sit and mope at home.

All he did was get his dole

and smoke his dope.

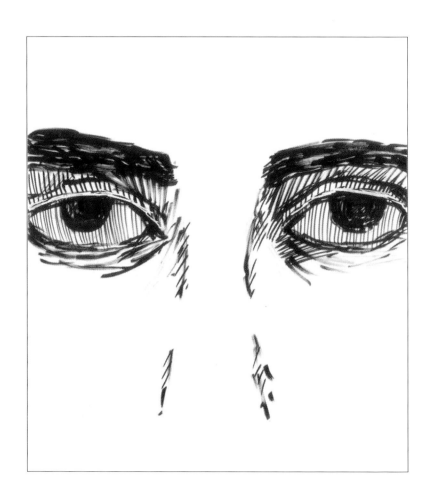

When he got stoned, it was no fun.
I knew he was on the ropes.
I knew he was alone -
and I felt bad for him.

But at the same time,
my girl, Rose, got pregnant.
We had a new home to get into.
We had a new home to make.

Then my dad died
and my mum broke down.
I had so much to cope with,
I could not cope with Jake as well.

I let a few weeks slip by.
Then I got the news
that Jake was in hospital.
He fell in the lake...

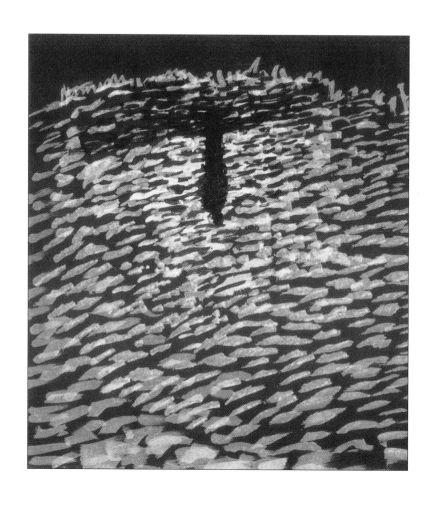

Was it an accident
or did he jump?
I still do not know.

He was in a bad state when I saw him.

He spoke like a madman.

It was no joke.

He made a grab for my hand.
He said his name was Mike,
not Jake.
He said Jake had died in the lake.

I felt a chill go through my bones.
Mike was Jake's twin brother.

One Christmas,
when they were six,
the lake froze.
Kids went to skate on the ice.

But the ice broke
and Mike fell in the hole.
They had no rope and no hope
to get him out in time.

Jake had said
he could not remember that day.
Now the same fate came for him.

When I went back to the hospital,
Jake was not there.
I went to his home
but his mum said he had left.

Jake had left Mudlake.
He left no note to say goodbye
and he left no trace.

Chapter 3

Life went on.

From time to time

I thought of Jake -

lost, alone and on the streets.

Nine years came and went.
Then one night
we had the TV on.
"Here!" Rose said, "Is that Jake?"

And it was.

Jake had made a name for himself.

He had it in him to write.

I got a book of his and read it.

It was a book about a family
and they did not get on.
It was about the things people think
when they are alone -

and the things people hide.
The Jake that I knew
could not write like that.

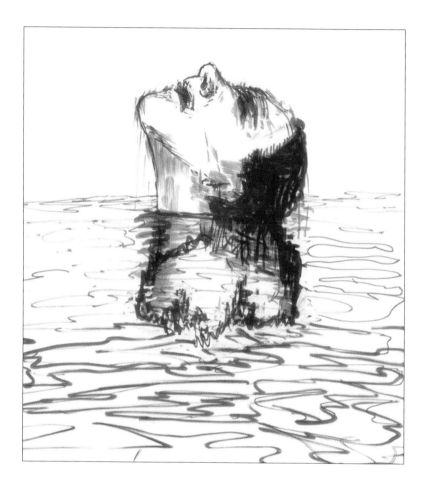

But did I know him?

Did I know what he was like?

Jake fell in the lake...

but did the same man rise from it?

I sent him a letter
and I got a line back.
Not from him -
but from his wife.

He had a thing
at this big bookshop in town.
We would dine at their hotel after,
she said.

With my glass of fine wine,
I thought - that's not bad
for a mate of mine!

He had a nice wife,
a nice job,
a nice life.

But the man at the end of the line
did not dress like Jake,
did not act like Jake.

He would not ride in the lift.

He went white

like he saw a ghost

and ran off down the steps.

While we ate,
his wife was all smiles.
But Jake did not say much.
He wanted to be rid of me.

All that time we were mates
and he did not want
to remember it.

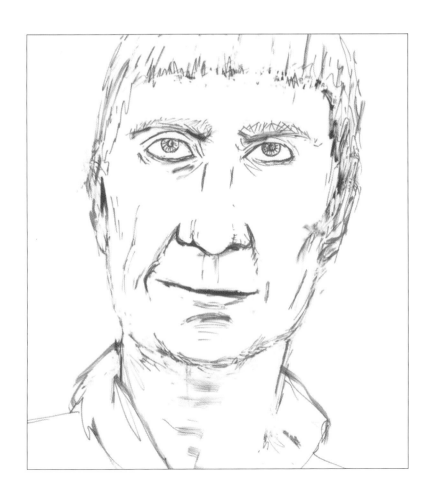

That's what fame does, I thought.
No time for your mates back home.
No time for the likes of me.

In the end, I gave up.

"Goodbye Mike... sorry, Jake!" I said.

I do not know why I made the slip,
but he did not pick up on it.

"See you then," we said
at the same time.
As if!

Chapter 4

Till the end of June,
I had the same bad dream.

It was like a tune on the jukebox
that goes over and over.

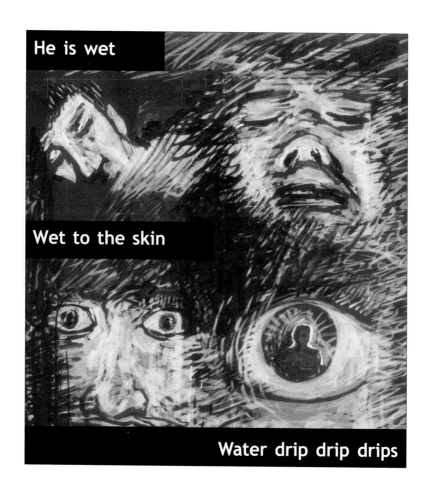

He is wet

Wet to the skin

Water drip drip drips

A man sits mute
at the end of my bed.
He has his back to me.
I know it's Jake.

He shakes with cold

His teeth chatter

I do not want him to face me.
Just as I think it,
he slowly turns.
My own scream woke me.

As a rule, I'm not like that.
As a rule, I refuse to think
there are such things...

but I felt haunted
by the ghost of Jake
- or the ghost of his brother.

I felt haunted...
and there was no refuge.

Then, in late June, a huge shock
put a stop to all of it.
My boys went on a bike ride
and Luke got hit by a van.

In the hospital,
when I held Luke's hand as he slept,
when I held his brother as he wept,
I saw how it was for Jake.

Till then, it had been about me.

How Jake left me.

How Jake had been rude to me.

How Jake had let me down.

But on that day, I saw how he felt.
All the things that haunted Jake
came from Mudlake
- and so did I.

I was on the same page as the rape,

the lake,

the loss of life,

the loss of innocence.

He had to rip it out
and make a new life.

Chapter 5

And then...

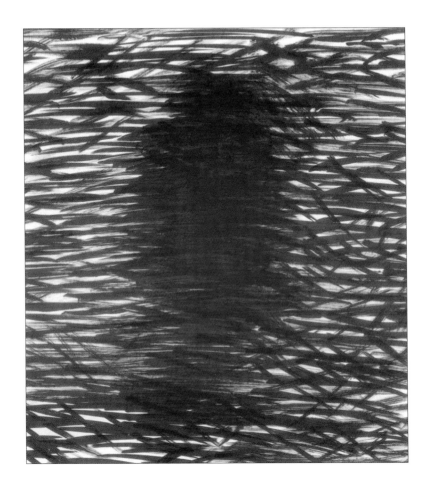

just five days after Luke's accident,
they got a body from the lake.

It was Dale.

He was last seen
in the Duke's Head up town.
He spoke to a man,
but no one saw the man's face.

Maybe it was a fluke,
but that same night,
I saw Jake get on a tube
near Mudlake.

At least, I think it was Jake.

He was dressed like he used to do
and his face was shaven.

He did not stop or wave
but, as he left,
he came to face me.
He met my eye as he went away.

I think we made a truce - an end.
From then on,
I had no bad dreams.

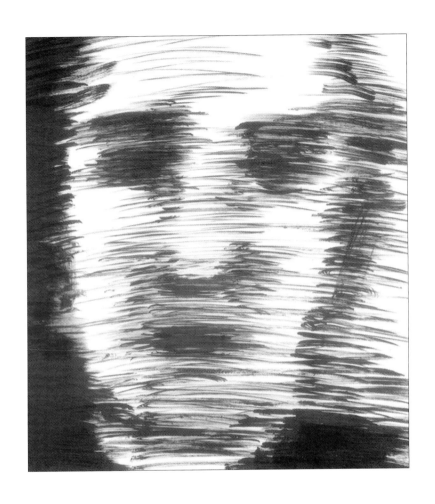

I did not tell the cops about Jake.

Like I said,

I only think I saw him.

I bet a lot of people
had it in for Dale.
It could have been Jake
or Pete or Jude.

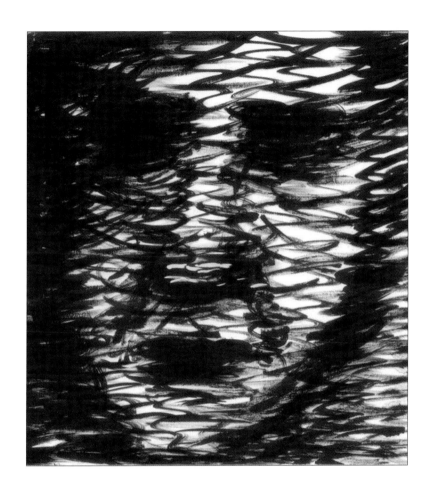

It could have been the ghost -
the face in the lake.

Or maybe Dale just got drunk
and fell in the lake all by himself.
That's what the cops had it down as.

But I'm glad that Dale met his end.
All he did in his life
was use and abuse people like Kim.

I hope Kim is happy now.
I hope Jake is happy too.
This much I do know -

you don't need ghosts
to be haunted.
But if there are ghosts,
let them rest.

Still, I remember Jake.

Still, I miss him.

THE END

Gatehouse Books®

Gatehouse Books are written for teenagers and adults
who are developing their basic reading and writing skills.

The format of our books is clear and uncluttered. The
language is familiar and the text is often line-broken,
so that each line ends at a natural pause.

Gatehouse Books are widely used within Adult Basic
Education throughout the English speaking world. They
are also a valuable resource within the Prison Education
Service and Probation Services, Social Services and
secondary schools - both in basic skills and ESOL
teaching situations.

Catalogue available

Gatehouse Media Limited
PO Box 965
Warrington
WA4 9DE

Tel/Fax: 01925 267778
E-mail: info@gatehousebooks.com
Website: www.gatehousebooks.com

Mudlake is a phonic adult beginner reader which focuses on the long vowel sounds.

A comprehensive set of tutor resources, mapped to the Adult Literacy Core Curriculum, is available to support this book.

Mudlake Tutor Resources
ISBN: 978-1-84231-028-1

Also available in the phonics series:

Sam The Man
ISBN: 978-1-84231-022-9

Sam The Man Tutor Resources
ISBN: 978-1-84231-023-6

NOTES

NOTES

NOTES

NOTES